THIS MAGI BOOK BELONGS TO :

_____

_____

_____

_____

For my good friends,
Sue, Liz and Irene
~S.C.

For Aaron
~T.L.

Reprinted 1998

MAGI PUBLICATIONS
22 Manchester Street, London W1M 5PG

This paperback edition published 1998
First published in Great Britain 1998

Printed in Italy by Grafiche AZ

ISBN 1 85430 448 8

Look Out
for the
Big Bad Fish!

by **Sheridan Cain**

illustrated by **Tanya Linch**

Magi

Tadpole swam in and out of the lily pads. It was warm and he wanted to splish and splash as never before.

"Hello, Tadpole," said Mother Frog
as she flopped on to a nearby lily pad.
"What a beautiful summer's day!"

"What's summer, Mum?" asked Tadpole.
"Summer is when the sun shines," said
Mother Frog. "We leap and jump
about because we're happy."

Boing

went Mother Frog.
She leapt high
into the air,
somersaulted
and landed
with a PLOP!

"I bet *I* can do that," said Tadpole
and he tried to leap on to the
lily pad where Mother Frog sat.
But all he could do was
splish and splash.

"Mum, why can't I jump like you?"
asked Tadpole.
"Oh you will, Tadpole, you will," said
Mother Frog.
"But I want to jump *now*," said Tadpole.
"When you are a little older, you will,"
she said.

Disappointed, Tadpole swam off downstream.
"Take care, Tadpole!" called Mother Frog.
"Look out for the Big Bad Fish!"

Tadpole wiggled his way to the edge of the
stream. Here among the kingcups it was safe.
"Hello," said a voice from high above him. Tadpole
looked up and saw a woolly face with a smudgy nose.

"Hello," said Tadpole.
"Who are you?"
"I'm Lamb," said the woolly face.
"Can you jump?" asked Tadpole.
"You bet I can!" said Lamb. "Watch this!"

Boing

went Lamb.

"Phew!" said Tadpole.
"I wish I could jump
like that."
"Oh you will, Tadpole," said
Lamb. "When you are a
little older, you will."
"But I want to jump
now," cried Tadpole and
he swam sadly home.

A few days later, Tadpole went
downstream again. He reached the
water violets that tickled his tummy.
"Hello," said a voice from a little above him.
Tadpole looked up and saw a twitchy nose and
the largest pair of ears he'd ever seen.
"Hello," said Tadpole. "Who are you?"
"I'm Rabbit," said the animal with the
twitchy nose.

"Can you jump?" asked Tadpole.
"Can I jump?" said Rabbit.
"Watch this!"

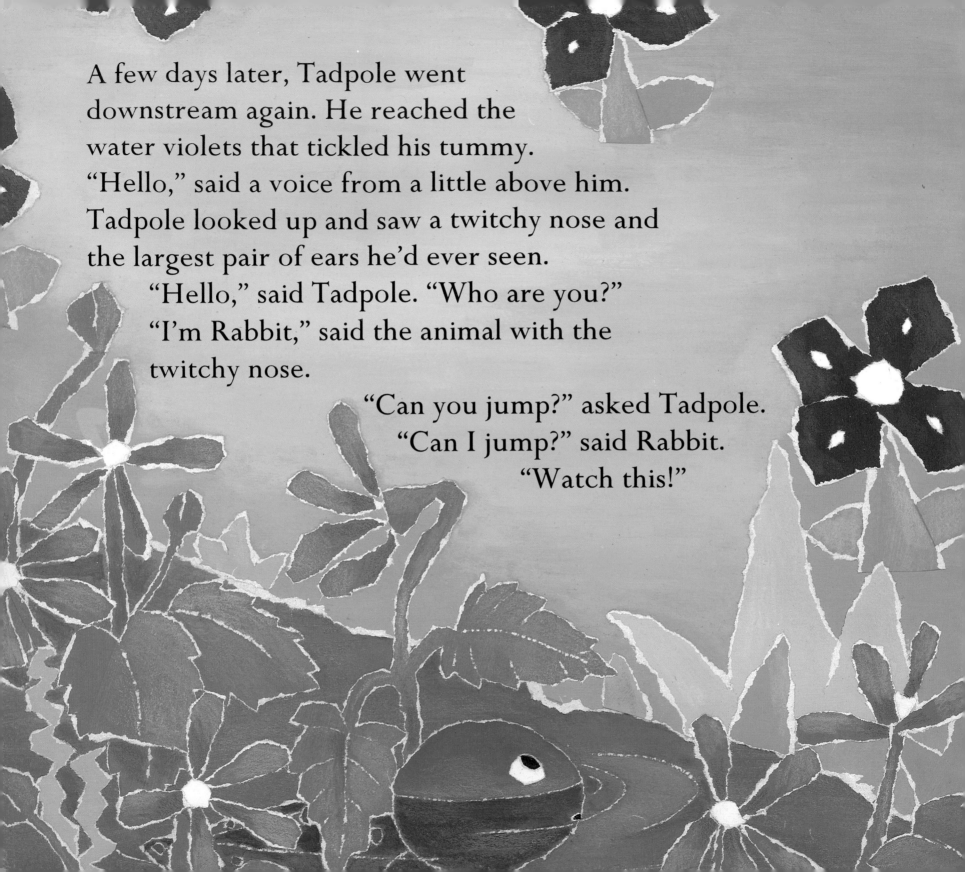

Boing

went Rabbit.

"Oh my," said Tadpole. "I wish I could jump like that."
"Oh you will, Tadpole," said Rabbit.
"When you are a little older, you will."
"But I want to jump *now*," wailed Tadpole and swam off home.

Several days later, Tadpole went out again.
This time he came across giant bulrushes,
wobbling in the wind and paddled towards them.
"Hello," said a voice in his ear. Tadpole looked
round. He saw a pair of bug eyes and two
springy legs.
"Hello," said Tadpole. "Who are you?"
"I'm Grasshopper," said the bug-eyed creature.
"Can you jump?" asked Tadpole.
"Of course," said Grasshopper.
"Watch this!"

Boing went Grasshopper.

"Wow!" said Tadpole. "I wish I could jump like that."
"Oh you will, Tadpole," said Grasshopper.
"When you are a little older, you will."
"But I want to jump *now*," wept Tadpole and swam off home.

The next time Tadpole went out,
he swam even further. The stream
widened and the water became clear.
"Hello," said a deep voice from below him.
Tadpole looked down and saw a pair of huge,
rubbery lips.
"Hello," said Tadpole. "Who are you?"
"I'm Big Bad Fish!" boomed the rubbery-lipped
   creature.
   "C-Can you j-jump?" stuttered Tadpole.
   "NO, BUT I *DO* EAT TADPOLES,"
   said Big Bad Fish.

Boing

went Tadpole.

Tadpole leapt higher than Lamb.
He leapt higher than Rabbit.
He leapt even higher than Grasshopper.
He leapt all the way back home
to the lily pads.

"Look, Mum," said Tadpole.
"I *can* jump!"
"Well done!" said his mother.
"What did I tell you,
Little Frog?"

Some more books from
Magi Publications
for you to enjoy.

A.H. BENJAMIN
A DUCK SO SMALL
ELISABETH HOLSTIEN

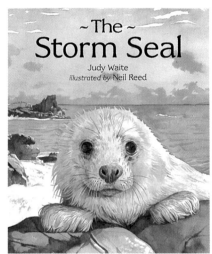

~ The ~
Storm Seal
Judy Waite
illustrated by Neil Reed

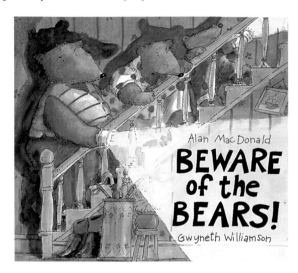

Alan MacDonald
BEWARE of the BEARS!
Gwyneth Williamson

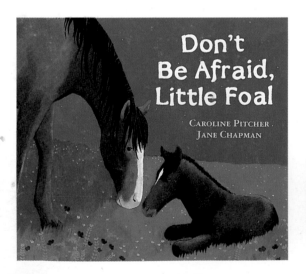

Don't Be Afraid, Little Foal
CAROLINE PITCHER
JANE CHAPMAN

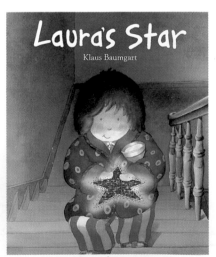

Laura's Star
Klaus Baumgart

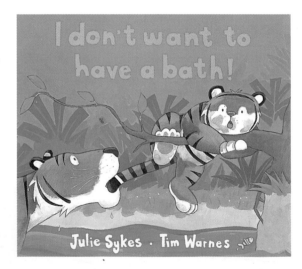

I don't want to have a bath!
Julie Sykes · Tim Warnes

All books available from most booksellers. In case of difficulty please contact
Magi Publications, 22 Manchester Street, London W1M 5PG, UK